Across the Delaware

Across the Delaware

AND OTHER STORIES OF LONG AGO
Compiled by the Editors
of
Highlights for Children

ISBN 0-87534-649-9

Highlights is a registered trademark of Highlights for Children, Inc.

CONTENTS

Across the Delaware

By Marcella Fisher Anderson

On Christmas night, December 25, 1776, James held his dog, Scout, close to him and raised his head above the side of the boat where he was hiding. Cargo rafts, ferries, and coal carriers crowded close to the Pennsylvania side of the Delaware River. James looked across to the New Jersey shore. Through the snow, he tried to see a candle shining in his mother's pantry window.

Suddenly, a strong hand grabbed his damp collar. "What are you doing here?" a sentry whispered harshly. "And a dog besides. Keep him quiet and follow me."

"I've only one mind, sir—to cross the river for home." James hurried to follow the sentry to his commanding officer.

"I found him, I did, on one of the boats, Sir. Give him your name, lad."

"James Morris." Remembering that his father had fought bravely against the British and died at White Plains, James added, "American patriot."

The officer's gaze softened. "Well, James Morris, you have discovered us in the midst of a surprise crossing of the Delaware tonight. You will have to come with us."

"Scout and I have crossed this river many times."

"Muzzle that dog, O'Hara," the officer said to the sentry, "and put them both next to the helmsman on the first boat. Young Morris may be useful."

In the stern of the boat, James rubbed Scout's nose where the rag strip was tied to keep him from barking. James thought of home and the October day he and his mother had learned of his father's death. Soon afterwards, his mother had sent James across the river to her parents' farm, thinking the change would be good for him. But James knew now that it had been the wrong thing for him to do. He had never fully faced the fact of his father's death. Now, he was afraid to go home—afraid to face the empty chair and the dark hearth where his father had always built a high fire, a better one than James felt he could ever make. James was sure of that.

"A fine way to spend Christmas night," said the helmsman quietly, interrupting James's thoughts. "A hard crossing even with us fishermen from Marblehead manning the boats."

"Where did all the boats come from?" asked James softly.

"Captain Daniel Bray and his men," whispered the helmsman. "On Washington's orders, they stole the boats at night, floated them downriver here, then hid them. Twenty-four hundred men are crossing tonight. We'll thrash those British at Trenton."

James heard the clatter of horses coming aboard, then felt a lunge beneath him as the boat was poled out onto the river. "The current will be swiftest closer to the other shore," he warned the helmsman.

Scout stirred in James's arms. Presently, a faint glow shone from Johnson's ferryhouse dead ahead. Close to land now, the Marbleheaders fought against the current.

As the boats scraped the stony bottom, men in the dark reached for the mooring lines. James stared. "Tories!" he said aloud. He recognized them as his mother's neighbors who supported England's king. James's heart stopped.

"It's no treachery, young Morris," said one of the men, grasping a horse's bridle. "The British have betrayed us. They burned my house last night. We're Americans now. Except for Krock. Strange one, he is."

James watched sentries run up the hill and disappear into the woods, but he knew that Krock could evade them.

Leaving Scout unmuzzled and snuffling about the guarded ferryhouse, James started tracking the Tory.

Snow alternated with sleet. A strong wind carried the sound of a church bell. One in the morning. The crossing had taken longer than planned, moving the surprise attack into daylight hours. James's head throbbed.

Two miles, from tree to tree, he followed Krock until at last the Tory headed for the ice-covered rock ledges that James himself climbed in summer to take a short cut to Trenton.

James circled swiftly around the rocks, reaching the ledges just as Krock stretched for one last handhold. He stepped on the man's hands. "Up or down, Tory?" James's heart pounded. What would he do now?

The man's lips parted over his teeth. "Rebel trash," Krock muttered as he tried to free his hands.

There was a movement in the woods below, and suddenly a brown bundle of energy growled its way up the rocks and leaped, fastening itself onto the man's ankle.

Krock's eyes widened in surprise. "Off, fiend!" he cried, losing his handhold and grazing the rocks as he fell backward onto the snow below.

James tore down and around the ledges, reaching the man as he staggered to his feet and rocked unsteadily. "March, Tory," James said, prodding the dazed man with a sharp, heavy stick he had seized.

"The rebels will not succeed tonight," Krock laughed, swaying a little. "Their muskets are too wet to fire." He twisted his head and spat at James's feet.

James prodded him harder in the ribs. "Back to the river, traitor."

From Johnson's ferry-house, the lanterns shone with an icy brilliance. Krock lunged to escape. James stretched out his stick and tripped him.

The Tory struggled to regain his footing but slipped on the ice-crusted snow. With a bellow, he rolled helplessly down the hill to the river. Scout and James ran beside him.

A familiar sentry rushed from behind the ferry-house. "Guard him, O'Hara," James shouted with triumph that rang in the frozen air. "He's a spy. I know him well!"

Soon, in the early light, James slogged wearily for home. He paused at his father's garden, where dry cornstalks rattled in the wind. He thought about the times he and his father had laughed and hidden from each other in the rows of tall corn. Remembering brought hot tears to James's eyes.

But James took a deep breath and, with Scout following, crossed the yard toward the candle in the window. It was time to be here to help his mother, time to face the empty chair and the hearth. James knew he could do that now.

It was time to be home.

••

The successful surprise attack against the British at Trenton was the first victory for the American Army and restored confidence in the American cause for independence.

All characters mentioned are fictitious, except for Captain Daniel Bray and General George Washington.

The Trailside Rocker

By Jean E. Doyle

The little rocking chair would have to go. Sarah could understand why, but she had to blink hard to keep back her tears.

Her father carried the beautiful chair to a big pile by the trail's edge. Her grandfather had given it to her just four years earlier.

The rocker had become her most prized possession. But the covered wagons had been weakened by the hard journey over the rough prairie trail. Now the wagons had to lighten their loads for the long miles yet to go.

A crude sign was stuck on top of the furniture and tools. It read: HELP YOURSELF. Those following were welcome to take whatever they could carry.

The wagon train started moving again. As they passed the pile, Sarah caught sight of the cradle that belonged to the Warrens. Their baby had died of the fever a hundred miles back and was buried beside the trail. Suddenly Sarah's own sacrifice didn't seem so great.

At last they reached Willow Springs. They celebrated the end of the long journey with a party. Then the families set about choosing their claims.

"Will we have a log cabin?" Sarah asked her father.

"There aren't enough trees around here," he told her. "Our first home will have to be a sod house. Maybe someday we can build a wooden house after we are settled in."

Sarah and her younger brother and sister helped to build the "soddie," as the little house was called. It was hard work cutting out the big "bricks" of sod and grass and then stacking them to make walls.

The door and the window frames were made of wood saved from old packing boxes. The roof was made from saplings cut down near the creek and covered with brush and more sod bricks.

It was a sturdy house that kept out the hot prairie sun. It was a bit damp inside, but comfortable.

Sarah and Ann Marie and Jonathan helped their parents on the claim. There were so many chores to do on those first days that there was little time left for play.

One day in late summer Sarah said to her mother, "I wish another family would move in closer than the Browns. It's hard to walk five miles to visit another girl my age."

Her mother smiled knowingly. "Mrs. Brown told me about a new family who staked a claim near the creek."

Sure enough, several days later they spotted a white-topped wagon making its slow way through the tall prairie grass. And when their new neighbors came to borrow some flour, Sarah met Lettie Dawson who was also ten years old. They liked each other at once.

Because of their many chores the girls could get together only on Sundays. At first Lettie came to Sarah's soddie to play. Her father had to clear some land before he could begin building theirs. But at last Lettie invited Sarah to spend the day at her new house.

The minute Sarah entered Lettie's new soddie she could tell it was a happy place. Checked curtains hung at the two small windows. A braided rug lay in front of the small fireplace.

And the furniture! There seemed to be much more than in Sarah's soddie. The Dawsons must have had a big, strong wagon.

She soon became used to the dim light inside the soddie after her long walk in the bright prairie sunshine. A soft crying drew her eyes to a corner of the room.

"It's just Jason," said Lettie as she she went to a cradle and lifted out her baby brother.

Then Sarah's eyes caught sight of another piece of furniture by the cradle. It was a small, beautifully carved child's rocker. She went to it at once. Could it be her grandfather's rocker, which she'd had to leave by the trailside months before?

Lettie saw her looking at the rocking chair. "Isn't it beautiful?" she asked. "I found it on a pile of furniture along the trail. My father said I could take it because someone else had to leave it behind. I sit in it every day when I sing little Jason to sleep. Whoever had to leave it behind really must miss it."

"I'm sure they do," Sarah agreed, moving quickly away. It wouldn't be right to tell Lettie that she was the one who had to give it up. At least now she knew it wasn't being rained on.

One October Sunday the girls decided to have a picnic. Sarah brought Anne Marie and Jonathan along while Lettie carried Jason.

The children found a beautiful spot under the willows by the spring. Soon the air would turn cold and snowstorms and cold winds would end their weekly visits until spring.

After eating, Sarah and Lettie lay back on the grass and talked about their old homes. Anne Marie and Jonathan floated stick boats in the shallow creek while little Jason crawled about investigating everything he could reach.

Suddenly the quiet afternoon was shattered by screams from Anne Marie and Jonathan. "Rattler! Rattler!" they warned and ran back to their older sister.

Baby Jason—where was he? Lettie looked around frantically. In her daydreaming she had neglected her responsibility. She jumped to her feet and ran toward the creek. She stopped short and stared spellbound when she saw Jason sitting just three feet from a coiled rattlesnake!

Sarah was right behind her. She spotted a big rock near her foot and quickly picked it up.

Please, God, don't let me miss, she prayed silently. Then she flung the rock at the snake's head. The snake seemed stunned, its rattle stilled. Sarah ran to Jason and quickly gathered him in her arms.

The four older children were still trembling when they returned to the Dawson soddie. When Mrs. Dawson heard about the frightening adventure, she hugged her youngest child until he squealed to be let down.

"We will never be able to thank you enough," she told Sarah with tearful eyes.

The next morning Jonathan shouted, "There's a wagon coming!"

Sarah saw the Dawsons approaching. Why were they visiting on a Monday?

Mrs. Dawson climbed down from the wagon and said to Sarah, "We have something for you."

Sarah's eyes opened wide as Lettie handed down the trailside rocker.

"I have nothing else worth giving," she said. "You must have it."

Sarah protested, "Oh, no! You love it so."

"I know," Lettie answered, "but my baby brother is worth more to me than a piece of furniture. Please take it."

Sarah looked at her mother who nodded. Only then did she reach out and accept the return of her beloved grandfather's gift.

After the Dawsons had left, Sarah went to a chest and took out the little patchwork pillow her grandmother had made.

"There," she said softly as she placed the pillow on the seat of her rocker. "Now you're both back where you belong."

Paul Cuffe
and the
Dream That Came True

By Dorothea Kent

Paul Cuffe gazed out to sea from his home on Cuttyhunk Island off the coast of New Bedford, Massachusetts. The sight of great-sailed ships on the horizon fascinated him. The sound of waves breaking on the shore exhilarated him, and he dreamed of one day going to sea as captain of his own ship.

When Paul was ten, his African-born father moved the family to a farm on the mainland near Westport. A former slave, Paul's father had worked hard, earned enough money to buy his freedom, and had married a Wampanoag woman. Since his father had made his dream of becoming a free man come true through hard work, Paul felt he should be able to realize his dream, too. His father always said, "Don't give up on something you want, and don't get angry. That only slows you down."

His father died when Paul was fourteen. Paul felt his dream vanishing, since his nine brothers and sisters and his mother needed him to work on the farm.

Two years later his brothers decided they could manage without him. Paul could try his luck at sea! Joyously, he walked to New Bedford. He strolled along the wharves, smelling the good ship smells of tar and fish until he spotted a whaler. He spoke to a sailor who asked him, "Are you a runaway?" (In those days most blacks in America were slaves.) Then he faced the captain, whose first question, also, was, "Are you a runaway?" Anger stirred within him, but he remembered his father's wise words.

The captain hired him. The ship sailed to the Gulf of Mexico. On their return the crew learned that the colonies were at war with Great Britain. On their way to hunt more whales, a British warship bore down upon them. All aboard were captured, taken to New York, and held prisoner there for three months.

After the war, Paul and his brother David built a small, single-sailed boat. Loading it with goods to trade, Paul set out for Cuttyhunk. Before long a large boat came alongside him. A pirate ship! Two of the pirates seized him. A third growled, "Get rid of him!" Tossed overboard, Paul came up to find his boat gone. Thinking of his father's words— "Don't give up!"—he swam the three miles to shore. He fell exhausted on the beach, extremely glad to be alive.

He worked evenings for many months building another boat, a two-sailer. Finally he set off for Nantucket Island with more goods to trade. Suddenly—he could hardly believe his eyes—a pirate boat! This time he managed to outrun it but ran onto a reef and had to go back for repairs. On his next try he succeeded in reaching the island.

Besides continuing his sea trade, Paul also supported his family's farm. He paid taxes on the farm, even though blacks weren't represented in the government. In 1780, he and his brother John wrote to the state legislature, asking for the same voting rights as white taxpayers. Many months passed and nothing happened. Finally, in 1783, the lawmakers decided that any taxpayer, black or white, could vote. This brought great joy to the free blacks of Massachusetts. Indeed, Paul may have been the first black American to make a successful appeal for the civil rights of blacks.

In 1783, when he was twenty-four, Paul married a Native American woman, Alice Pequit. By that time he owned an eighteen-ton schooner on which he brought cod from Newfoundland to Westport, where it was salted and packed for shipping. He soon had two more boats built, a twenty-five-ton vessel and another of forty-two tons.

When his children reached school age, there was no school near his farm. He suggested to his white neighbors that they should all get together and build a school, but no one else seemed interested. So he hired workers to build a one-room schoolhouse on his own land, which was near town and next to the road. He hired a schoolmaster and announced that all the neighborhood children could attend. Most of them did.

In 1793 Paul returned to whaling, setting out with two of his own boats. By the early 1800s he owned the 260-ton *Alpha* and a half interest in the two-masted, square-rigged brig *Traveller.*

The position of free blacks was precarious. They were sometimes claimed as slaves. Southern slaveholders resented them because the southern slaves wanted their freedom, too. And most jobs were given to white people. When Paul learned that some free blacks were considering making their home outside the United States, he sailed to the newly formed British colony of Sierra Leone in West Africa. England had recently outlawed slavery, and the colony was for free blacks. Paul traveled to London to get permission to take some black Americans to the colony. He returned home in 1812 to find that the United States and England were once again at war.

It wasn't until the war was over that he was allowed to take thirty-eight black men, women, and children to Sierra Leone. Most of them didn't have passage money, so Paul lent it to them. They landed in Freetown fifty-five days after embarking. Then he returned for another group.

He received hundreds of letters from blacks. Almost two thousand signed up to go. But Paul became sick and then died in September 1817.

He was buried near the Quaker Meeting House in Westport. The inscription on his tombstone reads:

In memory of
CAPTAIN PAUL CUFFE
a self-made man
Patriot, Navigator, Educator
Philanthropist, Friend
A Noble Character

A
Daughter's
Gift

by Carol M. Harris

Kapkap Ponnmi followed her father's gaze to
the valley and the blue waters of Lake Wallowa,
Oregon. Cascading mountain streams sparkled in
the June sun of 1877. When he spoke, Chief Joseph's
words were solemn.

"I have given up this land of my father's grave,
my daughter," he said. "The white men say we
must give it to them. Our young braves resist and
talk of war. But I am Chief. The decision is mine. I
want no Nez Perce or white blood to be shed. We

must leave our home and go to Lapwai reservation in Idaho. The white general has given us only thirty days to prepare." He walked away, his broad shoulders slumped.

Kapkap helped the women pack household goods for travel. As Chief Joseph's eldest daughter it was her duty to show a good example. But as she worked her resentment grew. How could white men claim this land for themselves when generations of Nez Perce had lived, worked, and been buried here?

On their final day, she went to the shore of the lake. She clutched her prized possession, a small, colorfully embroidered, beaded drawstring bag. She looked once again at the scene before her and drew it in her memory. Kneeling, she scooped a handful of earth into the bag.

"Someday," she vowed, "my father shall again see this land of his father and his father's father."

Kapkap hid her terror as she and her people crossed the turbulent Snake River on flimsy rafts of buffalo hide. In the evening, when they had set up camp, warriors rode up and reported that young braves from a neighboring band had killed some whites. They were seeking revenge because a white man had killed one of their fathers.

"The soldiers have already set out to find us," the warriors said. "We must be prepared to fight."

Elders gathered at her father's tepee. "Why should we fight?" Kapkap heard some say. "What does this have to do with us? Those braves are not of our band."

"But they are Nez Perce," Chief Joseph declared. "We are one tribe, after all."

All the other chiefs and warriors nodded their heads in agreement.

Everyone respected Chief Joseph. He was not a warrior. He was a man of peace, but first and foremost he was a Nez Perce.

"Chief Joseph says the soldiers will punish all Nez Perce for the killing," the women murmured. "He says all bands must unite and flee."

Kapkap wondered why white men had never been punished for their cruelty to the Indians. As she hurried to repack their belongings she held the beaded bag close to her heart. It was even more precious now.

Soldiers pursued them through canyons and valleys. Twice they attacked the struggling band of refugees. Kapkap applied herbs to the wounds of the injured, gathered camus bulbs to dry for food, and cared for the sick. She hated the roar of the soldier's guns and the look of pain on Chief Joseph's face as he walked among his suffering people. Like him, she was proud of their warriors' bravery.

But her soul was wounded each time a Nez Perce was hurt or killed.

Finally, there came a time when it seemed the soldiers were as weary of fighting as they. All was quiet as they traveled through the Bitterroot Mountains and set up camp. For the first time in months braves hunted buffalo instead of soldiers. Kapkap sat by the steaming kettles of meat and watched the warriors dance.

"Perhaps we will go home now," she whispered.

When she lay down to sleep Kapkap dreamed she was running swiftly as a deer along the peaceful banks of Lake Wallowa.

Suddenly, bursts of rifle fire pierced the quiet. Bullets tore holes in the tepee. Snatching her blanket, Kapkap wrapped two children in it and raced outside. Thick smoke and the smell of gunpowder filled the air. Horses whinnied with fear. She grabbed a spotted pony and threw the children onto its back. Climbing behind them she rode to the safety of a nearby stand of trees.

Hours later the battle sounds dimmed. Kapkap heard a great wailing. Her people were burying their dead.

The wounded grew weaker. Many died as they continued the difficult trek through the mountains of Montana.

"You have been courageous, my daughter," Chief Joseph said as they stood by the horses in their camp at Bear Paw Mountain on October 5. "The fighting should be over at last. We are near our friends, the Sioux, in Canada."

But again, with no warning, rifle fire broke the morning's calm. Soldiers rode into their midst, shooting wildly. Chief Joseph caught one of the horses and flung Kapkap onto its back. "Ride for your life!" he shouted to his daughter. As the nervous animal pawed the ground, Kapkap tugged at the cord that held her drawstring bag around her waist. "Wait!" she cried, "I have something for you." But it was too late. Chief Joseph rode off to join his warriors.

Kapkap escaped northward with a small group of women and children. After many days her cousin, Yellow Wolf, joined the weary wanderers. He told of the last battle the outnumbered Nez Perce had fought against the soldiers. He repeated Chief Joseph's words of surrender.

"I am tired of fighting . . . the little children are freezing to death . . . my heart is sick and sad. From where the sun now stands, I will fight no more forever."

For the first time Kapkap wept—for her father, her people, and herself.

She spent a harsh winter in Canada with the Sioux. She was not allowed to join Chief Joseph, who had been banished to Washington, separated forever from his family and his ancestral land.

Kapkap lived the rest of her life at Lapwai Reservation. She never saw her father again. But she sent him a package . . . a photograph of herself inscribed, "To Chief Joseph from his loving daughter" . . . and a faded, worn, beaded drawstring bag.

It is said that Chief Joseph often smiled as he gazed at the photograph and sifted the earth from his beloved Wallowa Valley through his fingers.

In Joss's Heart

By Heather Klassen

"Tomorrow, Joss, you'll join me when we go out to sea to fish," Joss's father declared. "I've been waiting for the day my son could join my crew since you were just a lad."

Joss looked up at his father's smile. "Yes, Papa," he replied. But Joss couldn't smile in return.

"You may do as you wish today, Joss," his mother said after his father had gone. "Enjoy your last day at play before you become a fisherman."

31

Joss ran from the cottage and headed inland, away from the gusty winds of the Cornish coast. He ran from the sounds of the sea, the calls of the fishermen casting their nets. Joss ran past banks of gorse, ablaze with yellow blooms, and through the heather grabbing at his legs. Joss ran until he spotted the stone towers of the engine house, the black belches of smoke, and the piles of slag dotting the land. Joss flung himself onto a hill above the mine, where he could watch the miners emerge from the shafts, blowing out the candles on their helmets.

If only Papa understood, Joss thought. *If only he knew I don't love the sea. I wish to be underground, digging for tin in the dark passages.*

Listening to the steady chug of the pumping engines, Joss didn't hear the man approach.

"Hello, lad. I've seen you watching us before."

Joss jumped up and faced a smiling miner. The man had to be a miner—his clothes were streaked with mud and clay, and a thin dusting of black coated his skin.

"I often come to watch the miners," Joss answered. "Every chance I can," he added.

"Come again, I'll take you closer," the man said.

"I'd like that, but I can't. Tomorrow I start fishing with my father. But I don't want to," Joss admitted, the words rushing out as if the miner were a trusted friend. "Papa always says that a Cornishman's born with either a fisherman's net or a miner's candle in his hand. I know I'm not a born fisherman. I want to be a miner. But I can't tell Papa. He has his heart set on my joining his crew."

"I see," the man replied. "Well, come to the mine with me today. At least you can have a look around."

Joss nodded, but inside his heart leaped with excitement. To actually go to a mine!

"I'm Alun," the miner said.

"Joss," Joss replied.

Joss followed Alun down the hill to the engine house. He watched men shoveling coal into the furnace and listened to the hiss of steam. Then he and Alun walked to the entrance of the main shaft. Alun called down to the men below.

"Could I go down?" Joss asked.

"I couldn't take you without your father's permission," Alun replied. "It's dangerous enough down there for the men. You could miss your footing and fall down the shaft. Besides, it's hot and dark and the tin dust pricks your nose. How do you know you'd even like mining?"

"I know I could handle a pick and hammer as well as any miner," Joss said. "I know how to spot the rock with flecks of white that tells you there's tin. I'm not afraid of earthfalls, either."

"You know quite a bit about mining for a fisherman's son," Alun said.

"I listen," Joss replied. "When the miners come to town, I listen to all they say."

"Perhaps you really are a born tinner," Alun said. "It's lunchtime. Share my sandwiches with me."

Glad for the offer, Joss followed Alun. But as he passed the miners coming up for their break, Joss remembered that this day would be his last at the mine. He would never go down the shaft and explore the maze of passages that reached out under the sea. Joss could barely swallow the bread Alun handed him because his throat was so tight with held-back tears.

"You know," Alun said. "To be a first-class miner requires years of apprenticeship."

Joss stared at Alun. "Are you saying I could be an apprentice?"

"I'm in charge here," Alun replied. "And you could if I say so. I think you have the makings of a fine tinner, Joss."

"But Papa . . ." Joss started.

"You'd make an honest day's wage," Alun said. "Perhaps he wouldn't object if you told him what's in your heart. Now I must go. I've been above far too long. I hope to see you again, Joss."

Joss watched Alun disappear down the shaft.

I need to get home, Joss decided. I need to talk to Papa. I'll tell him, really tell him, how the mine makes me feel. How it calls to me, like the sea calls to him. And that I have an offer of apprenticeship. Papa will have to let me try it. He could never let such an offer go by.

Joss stood up and gazed at the miners returning to their shift. *Soon,* Joss thought, *soon I'll be underground with them, exploring the candlelit tunnels, searching the rubble for hints of tin.*

Joss ran, not noticing the purple foxglove and tiny bluebells as he sped by. He had to hurry to speak to his father. Hurry to spill his heart. Joss smiled as he ran. He knew his father would listen and agree. He knew his father would never keep another Cornishman from his true desire.

The Snow Soldiers' Christmas

By Beth Thompson

The soft, white curves of the snowy Pennsylvania hills made it look like Christmas outside, but indoors, Abagail McDonald felt that the year 1777 would end with no Christmas at all. Her younger brother, Timothy, had brought in sweet-smelling pine boughs, but Abagail did not want to decorate the stone mantel this year, or have gifts, or anything . . . if Papa and Jonathan weren't going to be there to share it with them.

"Abby! Abby, come on out!" called Timothy from the snowy front yard where he was building a lopsided snowman. Abagail noticed that he had given it a branch for a musket and had made a tri-cornered hat, like his father's.

"Not now, Tim," she called back. As Abby watched, a small, brown bird perched for a moment on the snowman's bare branch and then flew away. "Little bird," she whispered, "fly to Valley Forge to tell Papa and Jonathan how much we miss them and how we long for the war to end." Abagail wished she could fly away with the bird.

Since her father and older brother had marched away to help General Washington win the war for independence for the American Colonies almost two years ago, Abby, Timothy, and their mother had worked as hard as any men to keep the farm going. But the two empty spaces at the table each evening reminded them all that the family was not together. With a sigh, Abagail turned away from the window and dutifully continued knitting a pair of mittens for Timothy's Christmas gift.

"Mama," she asked, for the third time that day, "isn't there *any* way to get our gifts to Papa and Jonathan?" Abby had long ago finished knitting two pairs of mittens for Christmas gifts. Now the gifts lay wrapped in calico in the cedar cupboard.

"I'm afraid not, Abby," sighed her mother. "These heavy snows have left the roads blocked. I'm not sure any of my letters have gotten through."

"Mama! Abby! Come quickly!" called Timothy. "The strangest snowmen ever! They're walking across our field!"

Abagail and her mother peered out the window at the small, snow-covered band of men marching toward the house. There were three men, dressed in tattered clothes and snowy rags. Their boot soles flapped, and Abby could see toes peeking through the holes in their socks. One man had no coat at all and wore a blanket tied around him. And another, not much more than a boy, had no gloves. He breathed upon his cold, blue fingers for warmth.

They were soldiers! Abby and her mother hurried out, desperate for news.

"Morning, ma'am," said one of the soldiers. "I'm Corporal Mason, and these are Privates James Tate and Johnny McCallum." The gloveless soldier grinned at Abby and Timothy. "Could we trouble you for a hot drink and a rest by your fire? We're on our way to join General Washington's troops at Valley Forge."

"Come in, come in," Abby's mother urged the men. "You need a hot meal. In fact, stay the night.

It's almost sundown now. Do you . . . do you have news of Valley Forge? My husband and son are there."

"No news, ma'am," said Corporal Mason, "except that rations are scarce. We'd be most happy to carry a message to your husband, if you'd like." He and the other soldiers eagerly spooned up hot stew, as Abagail and her mother bustled about cutting bread and adding wood to the fire.

"Could you take our Christmas gifts to them?" asked Timothy.

"We'd be happy to," said Johnny McCallum. "It's little enough to do to thank you for your warm hospitality." He wiggled his fingers before the fire.

That night, the three weary soldiers slept on blankets spread before the fireplace. Watching them sleep, Abby made a wish that Jonathan and her father were also warm this cold December night. It was then that the idea came to her.

"Mama, the soldiers are so kind to take our gifts and messages to Papa and Jonathan. Can't we find Christmas gifts for them, too?"

"Although I wish we could, Abby, we have so little time," said her mother worriedly.

"You could bake them an applesauce cake," suggested Timothy. "They can share it on the way. And I'll . . . I'll make them some snowshoes out of sapling twigs, the way Papa showed me. It will help them to walk through the heavy snow."

Abagail's thoughts went immediately to the cold, bare hands of Private McCallum. If she added more rows, the mittens she was knitting for Timothy would fit him. There would be time enough to knit another pair for her brother before Christmas morning. Abby smiled delightedly at the idea.

Then her mother surprised her. "Abby, bring me your old shawl and my sewing scissors." Abby brought them and then watched speechless as her mother cut the warm brown shawl into three long strips. "Mufflers," she explained to the bewildered children. "I'll bind the edges with blanket stitches."

Abagail was happy to see gifts had been found for all the soldiers . . . but what would she wear to keep warm? She stared out at the falling snow. And then she felt something wonderfully warm laid over her shoulders. "Merry Christmas, my dear daughter," said her mother. "It's early, I know, but it comes with love all the same. And I think you'll be needing it before Christmas Day!" It was a new shawl, knitted by her mother. It was deep blue and edged with red and brown stitches.

"Blue for your eyes," her mother explained, "brown for your lovely hair, and red to match your cheeks on these cold days."

Abby hugged her mother, happy tears falling on the new shawl. There was such a lovely feeling of peace in the house at that moment, with the firelight shining softly on the sleeping soldiers. Abby felt certain that her father and brother would be coming home again. She felt sure that General Washington would lead his men to victory and that Christmases to come would be celebrated in a free land. Softly humming a Christmas carol, Abby took out her knitting to finish the mittens for the smiling young soldier.

TWENTIETH-CENTURY PIONEERS

By Loverne Morris

"Andy, yesterday I sold cream to the sawmill workmen, and I plan to use that money to get a reader and speller so we can start your lessons."

"Mama, I wish I could go to school. Other children do."

"But Andy, the nearest school is at Heron, four miles away. No road, deep woods, and that Clark River crossing on the catwalk high above the water. How would you get through the snow in winter?"

"Why can't we have a schoolhouse here?"

As Andy spoke, his father came through the door saying, "Maybe we can. Dave Jones has offered two acres for a school site and Heron Schoolboard members say if we three families on this side of the river will build a schoolhouse and find a teacher, the board will pay the teacher and supply desks and books and a stove."

"Yea!" shouted Andy.

"Have you talked to the other men?" Andy's mother asked.

"I will today."

"Until we can grow gardens we will have to depend on trout, wild game, wild fruits, and greens for food. How will you find time to cut timber on those two acres?"

"We'll talk about that," Andy's father said.

He talked to the other men and they agreed that a school was needed. Each of the three families had two school-age children and younger ones who would soon reach that age.

The three families had just started wilderness homes in the Montana woods, a mile from the Idaho line, across the Clark Fork River from the lumber mill town of Heron.

They decided to build the schoolhouse, and a workday to clear the site was announced. Volunteers came from twenty miles around. The women made a picnic lunch, and by night the site was bare of trees. The very next day Andy's father and the other pioneers started building a one-room log schoolhouse. "We'll call it the Wilderness School," Andy's father said.

They found a teacher, and school began in September. Andy had to walk a mile and a half to school through pathless woods. He knew there were bears, deer, cougars, and lynx in the woods, but the mill workers told him if he did not threaten those creatures, they would not threaten him.

At school he became fast friends with a boy named Sam. They talked about their arrival in Montana the past spring. Their fathers had brought livestock and furniture by immigrant freight car to the end of the line at Cabinet, Idaho, and the women and children had come by passenger car. They spoke of how scary it had been to cross Clark Fork River on the ferry. They had dug pits in the snow to hold the horses and pigs and sheep until they could build brush shelters for them. Then log cabins and barns were built. Sam's family had lived in a tent during the building, but a logger had loaned his cabin to Andy's family.

That area had been cleared by loggers before 1910, and the boys found a log chute beside Blue Creek. Logs would be pushed down the greased chute into Blue Creek and the current would take them from Blue Creek to Clark Fork River and to Lake Pend O'Reille. There, men called river pigs would use pike poles to steer them to the sawmill. Andy and Sam agreed that they would not want to be river pigs.

Weeks galloped away. Andy learned his lessons well. Holiday time brought a Christmas party and program in the new log schoolhouse. The children decorated the Christmas tree by stringing colored paper loops and using wild berries and evergreens. Each child received a bag of cookies and candy.

"The best Christmas ever," said Andy.

Spring brought a May Day party to the school. The children brought wild flowers to class: blue and yellow violets, shooting stars, and wild roses.

Soon the term was over. Both the teacher and the children prepared a program for the end of school. Children recited poems and told stories. Then there was a feast shared with visiting lumberjacks. Andy's father had brought a box of apples and put it into a shed behind the schoolhouse. Andy's mother sent him to get some of the apples for the feast. As he approached the shed in the moonlight, he saw a dark moving form. A bear! Andy stopped as though turned to ice. Then he realized that the bear was after those precious apples. He must stop it. He thought fast. He had heard that bears hate noise. Quietly, Andy slipped back into the schoolhouse and whispered to Sam and each of the other boys. He said, "Bring lunch pails and spoons and anything you can bang!"

The boys slipped out the back door and began making a big racket, banging pails together and hitting pails with spoons.

Parents rushed out to see what the noise was about and got there just in time to see the bear retreating.

"A big black bear!" exclaimed Andy's mother. His father and the other men told Andy and the other boys, "Good for you! Making that racket was exactly the right thing to do!"

The years went by, and the school in the wilderness was the scene of many community activities as more and more settlers arrived. But no matter how times changed, the story of Andy and the children who scared away the bear was always a favorite at the school.

A Hard Road to Freedom

By Joan Strauss

The girl who stood on the doorstep was very different from what Amy expected. If Amy had been in her place, she would have cried. It must be frightening to leave your family to live with strangers. But this girl had a smile to match the sparkle in her brown eyes.

She nodded at Amy until her pigtails bounced. "I'm glad we're going to be sisters for a while."

"Thee must be very kind to Sarah," her mother had said in their Quaker way of speaking. "She has been a slave, but we have bought her freedom. She will stay with us until we can bring her family North, too."

Amy never paid much attention when her parents talked about slavery in the South and the war that might come. Their home in Philadelphia seemed very far away from it all. How sad to think a girl her own age was a slave!

Amy took Sarah's hand. "I'll be thy sister, and thee can sleep in my room."

"Not out back in the quarters?" Sarah asked.

"I don't know what quarters are, but it's too cold to sleep out back this time of year." Amy laughed at how silly that would be. Sarah laughed with her. It was fun to have a sister to giggle with!

Sarah went to school for the first time in her life. One snowy day, she and Amy came home to find a big wooden crate in the kitchen. Amy's mother was out, and nobody else was in the kitchen.

Curiously, the girls walked around the box. "Maybe somebody is sending us a wonderful present," Amy said.

"My big brother gave me a present once. A kitten," Sarah said, "but I had to leave it behind."

"Sarah?" A voice croaked from inside the box. The girls grabbed each other in fright. The voice came again. "Sarah! It's Jim! Get me out of here!"

Sarah screamed. "That's my brother! Jim! Jim! Are you a ghost?"

"No, girl, I'm in the crate. Get me out. Get a hammer and pull out the nails."

Amy ran to get a hammer. She had seen her father pry out nails many times.

"Loosen the bottom boards, so I can crawl out," Jim directed. It was not easy, but the thought of the boy shut up in the crate gave strength to Amy's hands. Frantically, the two girls worked until Jim could crawl through the opening they made.

He lay on the floor, taking deep gulps of air. Sarah was holding on to him and crying. "Why did they put you in the box? Why?"

Jim stretched his legs out carefully, as if afraid they would break. "To save me from the slave catchers. The underground railroad folks took me underneath a wagonload of hay to Mr. Garrett in Delaware. He sent me here in the box. Mr. Garrett says they had done that with other slaves. It isn't much fun, but the slave catchers didn't get me."

Jim rubbed one leg, and Amy noticed a cloth wrapped around it.

"How did you breathe?" Sarah asked.

"They put holes in the box. And they gave me a canteen of water." Jim looked around the kitchen. "But I could eat somethin'."

Amy quickly sliced bread and brought butter, milk, and cold meat from last night's dinner. Wincing with pain, Jim struggled to sit up.

"You're bleeding!" Sarah cried.

Jim looked down at his leg. "They set the hounds on me when I ran away. One of them caught me, but I tore loose. Mr. Garrett fixed me up as best he could. I reckon movin' around started it up again."

"I'm going for the doctor," Amy declared.

Jim struggled to stand up, but fell back. "No, don't! They'll take me back! Don't tell anybody! Just press on the bleeding like Mr. Garrett did."

Amy was already putting on her cape and boots. "I'll get Dr. Richardson. He's a member of the Anti-Slavery Society with my mother and father. He won't tell. Sarah, do what he says to stop the bleeding."

Amy had a weary trudge through the deepening snow, but Dr. Richardson bundled her into his buggy for the drive back.

"You did some quick thinking, young lady," he said after he had cleaned and bandaged Jim's wound. "If you had waited until your folks came home, he would have lost too much blood."

Amy went to bed that night so tired she didn't hear Sarah slip away before dawn.

"Sarah and Jim have gone, Amy," her mother told her when she awoke. "It was safer for them not to stay here. Slave hunters sometimes seize even freed slaves for reward money. Friends are taking Sarah and Jim to Canada."

"Does that mean I won't see Sarah again? She was my sister." Amy wanted to cry, but she remembered how cheerful Sarah was. Sarah didn't cry. Amy wouldn't, either.

"She will always be thy sister. We hope to send their mother and father to join them soon. It's a long, hard journey in the snow, but we pray they will make it in safety."

One day in June, long after the snow had melted, a letter with a Canadian stamp came for Amy.

"Dear Amy," the letter said. "I can write now. I am going to school. I am helping Jim learn how to read. My ma and pa are here. Write to me. Your sister, Sarah."

"Dear Sarah," wrote Amy, and she signed her letter, "Your sister, Amy."

THE GUEST ROOM

by Helen Kronberg

The doorbell rang. Karen rushed to the top of the stairs. "Come on up, Ellie," she yelled.

But it wasn't her friend, Ellie, at the door. Her mother was there, and she was talking to two men.

"A room?" Mother said. "I've never considered taking in roomers. We've only lived in this house for a few months."

One of the men snorted. "All these big houses and nobody has a room. The navy sent us to supervise at the rubber plant. Are we going to have to sleep in the car until the end of the war?"

Mother sighed. "We bought the house because of the guest room. A place for our parents when they visit. But come in. The room isn't big. But there are twin beds. There's only one bathroom," she added.

The men followed Mother upstairs. The tall one nodded at Karen as they passed her in the hall.

After the men had gone, Mother came back upstairs. "There goes the guest room," she said. "And you and Ellie will have to be a little neater. Keep your things in the toy room where they belong."

"Where will Grandma and Grandpa sleep when they come?" Karen asked.

Mother shrugged. "Where they slept in the other house. In our room. Your dad and I will be back on the sofa." She went to the linen closet and got out extra towels.

The men moved in within the hour. Karen went to tell Ellie about the two roomers.

"I love those cute Navy uniforms," Ellie said.

Karen laughed. "They don't wear uniforms. They work for the Navy. But maybe they're not *in* the Navy. Not like Uncle Chuck."

"Do you think they were at Pearl Harbor when the Japanese attacked?"

Karen shrugged. "How would I know? I didn't talk to them."

The men were not there much except to sleep. But once in awhile Karen was on the front porch when they came in. They talked to her and showed her pictures of their families. The tall one had a teenage daughter. The one called Mike had three boys.

"I think they're homesick," Karen told Ellie.

One day Aunt Irene was in the kitchen with Mother. Aunt Irene was crying.

"Was Uncle Chuck killed?" Karen whispered.

Her mother shook her head. "No. But why don't you check on your cousins, now? I let them go up to the toy room to play."

Karen took the stairs two at a time. Amy was five and Tony only two-and-a-half. They could not be trusted long by themselves.

"Hi, kids," she said. She gently moved the finger paints out of reach. "Here, try the crayons." She gave them each a sheet of paper. "How about making me a picture?"

When Mother called them down to eat supper, Aunt Irene was no longer crying. But her eyes and nose were red.

"Aunt Irene and the kids are going to stay with us," Mother said.

Karen gulped. "Where are they going to sleep?"

"Dad will help you carry things to the basement. And we'll have to use the toy room for an extra bedroom."

"The toy room! Mom, it's so tiny."

Mother nodded. "I know. There's no closet or anything. But we'll just have to share. Aunt Irene's cot and Tony's crib will go in there. We'll shove things together in your room for Amy's bed."

"I just feel so alone without Chuck," Aunt Irene said, sadly.

Dad patted her shoulder. "Nobody is really alone as long as there's family."

"We'll sure never be alone," Karen muttered under her breath.

"I want to sit by Karen," Amy said.

Karen got the kids onto their chairs at the table. They often had extra people for meals. But never had it seemed so crowded.

After supper Karen and Dad started clearing out the toy room.

"I'm sorry," Dad said as he put up shelves in the basement. "It won't be forever." He motioned for Karen to hold one end of the board. "Aunt Irene's sitter quit to work in the ammunition factory with her. The landlord, on the very same day, informed her he was letting a relative have their apartment."

Dad sighed and hammered in another nail. "It will be hard on your mother, too. But with both sitters and apartments just impossible to find . . ."

He didn't have to finish the sentence. Karen knew what he meant. Families help families. Especially when one of them is off fighting the war.

Karen's games stayed on the shelf. Painting was too risky with the kids around. Mostly she and Ellie played catch with Amy and Tony in the yard. They took them for walks or pushed them in the swing.

One day the guest room was empty. "The men have been called to San Diego," Mother said.

The war was over. Aunt Irene lost her job at the ammunition factory. And a few days later Uncle Chuck appeared at the door.

Uncle Chuck and Aunt Irene took the guest room. Tony had the toy room to himself. Grandma and Grandpa came to welcome Chuck home. They slept in Mother's and Dad's room. Aunt Maggie and Uncle Stuart came from Connecticut. They slept in a motel, but spent their days at the house.

An extra table was set up in the dining room. But it didn't seem crowded at all. The war was over, and they were all there to celebrate.

When a Boy of Seven Drove a Covered Wagon

By Loverne Morris

The trip started well enough. There were two covered wagons, and Pa had said, "Iven, you'll have to drive the second wagon. There's no one else to do it."

Pa had covered two large farm wagons by bending tall wooden bows across them and stretching canvas over the bows. They were filled with beds and tables and chairs and tools and food—all things for a new home.

Before Pa climbed into the lead wagon, he told Iven, "Your team will follow with no fuss. But I'll look back often to see that you're all right."

Iven felt proud but a little lonely as he sat on the high wagon seat. He slapped the reins, yelling, "Hi ya! Giddup." *Clop! Clop!* went the horses' hoofs, striking the hard dirt road. *Rumble* and *creak* sounded the wagons. Above Iven's head a lantern swung from a hook.

Iven's mother and sister and baby brother were traveling by train and would meet them in Wenatchee, halfway across the state of Washington.

The covered wagons rolled on, over dirt roads that ran between fields of wheat or stretches of wild grass. For miles and miles there were no houses. There were no trees, but Iven did not miss them. He had lived on a wheat ranch with not a tree in sight from the house. He was not used to trees.

Neither was he used to ravines, and he opened his eyes wide when he saw a great dry gulch ahead, deep and wide. His father stopped and came back to the second wagon to say, "This is the Grand Coulee. It's a dry wash, and the road down is not steep. It slants down so easy you won't need to set the brake on the wagon. Just follow me."

The way down was easy enough, but after the wide gulch was crossed, the horses strained to pull up the other side. They pulled hard, but the climb was slow, and his father's wagon got out of sight. Iven breathed a little fast. But when the team reached level ground at the top of the bank, Pa was there waiting. He said, "Smooth going ahead. I'll fasten the second wagon to the front wagon, and you can ride with me for a while."

Iven climbed up beside Pa and rode until it was time to camp for the night. While Pa made a campfire and cooked bacon and potatoes, Iven fed oats to the horses and then staked them out where they could eat grass. Soon it was dark. Iven and Pa rolled themselves up in their blankets and stretched out to sleep.

So far they had seen no one on the trip, but the next day Pa said, "We'll probably reach Preston Hanley's ranch this morning. He's an old friend of mine. If he's home, we'll visit."

Breakfast things were packed away, and Iven took his place in the second wagon. He began seeing small clumps of trees. Soon he saw fences and then a house and other buildings. A horseman came riding. Pa stopped and greeted him with a big handshake and clap on the shoulder. Iven figured this must be Preston Hanley. Pa swung down and came to the second wagon, saying, "Come along. The hired man will look after the horses."

Mr. Hanley shook Iven's hand and led the way to the house. The noon meal was cooking, and Iven sniffed all the good smells. Soon the food was on the table. Iven ate until he could eat no more. The men pushed back their empty plates and started talking about their boyhood in Wisconsin. Iven half-listened to the strange sound of leaves rustling in the wind. There were trees all around the house.

By midafternoon Pa said they must travel on. When the teams were ready, Mr. Hanley brought out a grand gift, a box of crisp, juicy, red apples. Iven ate one right away. Never before had he eaten an apple other than on Christmas or his birthday. "Eat another," Mr. Hanley said, and Iven did. Then Pa put the box of apples in his wagon, and they said good-bye to Mr. Hanley.

After two more days of travel, they came to the Columbia River. It was so wide that Iven could barely see the far bank. There was no bridge. There was a ferry, but it was so small it could take only one wagon at a time.

Pa told Iven, "You wait here while I take the first wagon across. I'll tie my team over there and come back for you and the second wagon."

Iven felt strange as the ferryman pushed off into the river with Pa and his wagon. An overhead cable shook, struggling to keep the ferryboat on course as the current tried to push it downstream. Soon the ferryboat looked no bigger than a toy, and then Iven couldn't even see it. The horses neighed and moved restlessly. The rushing river made a low roar. Iven felt tears pushing against his eyelids. Then he saw something moving, coming along the riverbank and stirring dust. He thought of wolves.

Then he saw that it was a herd of huge rams with curly horns. Driving them was the tallest man he had ever seen. He spoke to his two sheep dogs, ordering them to hold the flock, and then he came to Iven. He said, "Was that your pa I saw taking a wagon across the ferry?"

"Yes."

"And he's coming back for you and this wagon?"

"Yes." Iven's voice quavered.

"No worry," the man said. "Just takes a little time. You and I can visit until he gets here. How do you like my rams?"

"They're sure big!"

"Blue ribbon stock. Is your pa a rancher?"

"He had a big wheat ranch. Now we're moving to Wenatchee."

"A pretty town, Wenatchee. Lots of fruit—apples—and one man has a thousand acres of cherries."

The big shepherd stayed and talked with Iven until the ferry brought Pa back. The two men shook hands and talked briefly, then Pa climbed into the wagon beside Iven, took the reins, and drove the team onto the ferry. Iven looked back and the shepherd waved to him with his long staff, then turned to his rams.

It was Iven's first ferry ride, and the motion made him a bit dizzy. The sun on the water hurt his eyes, so he closed them. But he felt quite safe with Pa beside him. In a little while they docked on the west side of the river and Pa said, "Take a look. Over there is Wenatchee. I'll get my team, and we'll hurry down to the depot so that we get there before the train pulls in with your mom and your sister and your baby brother."

Iven was glad that their long journey had gone so well. He felt good in knowing how he had helped his pa, and now he was ready for his new life in Wenatchee.

THE UNEXPECTED JOURNEY

By Ann Bixby Herold

In colonial times some people came to America because they wanted to be free. Others came because they were hungry.

Methusala Evans came to America by mistake.

The morning Meth started on his unexpected journey he wasn't at all hungry. For breakfast he had eaten an egg, some bread, the remains of a pork pie, half a mutton chop, and two apples.

And he wasn't seeking freedom.

He was only twelve, but he had a job at the Sign of the Dancing Sailor, an inn in the port city of Bristol, England. Meth stabled horses, carried trays to the dining room, and ran messages.

He liked his life.

Travelers tossed him pennies when he fetched their horses. And if he was hungry, there were always leftovers like pork pie and mutton chops.

"You are a cheerful, hardworking lad," the innkeeper told him. "Your parents would be proud of you."

Talk of his parents made Meth feel sad. They had both died the year before. He had one sister. She was married and at first he lived with her. But when her husband apprenticed Meth as a clerk in a stuffy office, he ran away to Bristol.

In the note he left behind he said:

Clerking is not for me.
I am going to seek my fortune.

The innkeeper chuckled when Meth told him his name.

"Methusala? Didn't the Bible say he lived over nine hundred years?"

"Maybe I will, too," Meth said with a grin. "Then I'll have time to make nine fortunes instead of one."

The inn was busy that morning.

A sailing ship, bound for Philadelphia, was moored alongside the wharf at the end of Dock Street. The captain had been waiting all week for a fair wind. At last the wind was up and the tide was right.

Some of the *Nancy Brown's* passengers were staying at the inn. The innkeeper told Meth to put their luggage on a cart and deliver it to the ship.

The wharf was noisy with the shouts of the sailors and the thunder of unfurled sails. The air smelled of salt and seaweed and tar. The officer at the gangplank frowned at the luggage.

"It is late," he complained. "Every man jack on board this ship is manning the ropes. There is not a hand to spare."

"I'll carry it down to the cabins," Meth offered eagerly. The innkeeper hadn't said anything about hurrying back. Meth had always wanted to look over a ship, but he had never had the chance before.

"Hurry it up, then," said the officer.

It took a while to find the tiny cabins. It was dark below and they were tucked into corners. Meth squeezed past sad-faced passengers on their way back on deck for one last good-bye.

The luggage had been delivered to the cabins and no one had yet shouted "All ashore that's going ashore!" so Meth decided to explore the ship.

He found the storerooms and the galley, and the 'tween decks where the sailors' hammocks hung in rows.

"The wind must be stronger," Meth said to himself as the hammocks swung to and fro.

Suddenly, he noticed it was strangely quiet overhead. The only sound was the creak of timbers. He raced up on deck and stared about him in horror.

Gone was the busy wharf and Dock Street. Gone the row of moored ships. Bristol was a huddle of buildings fast disappearing into the distance.

"Let me off!" he cried.

They had passed the last of the ships at anchor. It was much too far to swim. The *Nancy Brown's* figurehead dipped gracefully to meet the open sea.

"STOP! Take me back!" The wind whipped the words away.

"There's no turning back, lad," a sailor called from the rigging. "Do you have money for your fare?"

One penny and an apple was all Meth had in his pockets.

"You may work off part of your passage," the captain said. "Your parents can pay the rest."

When he heard Meth was an orphan who had run away, he said, "I will have to find you work in the New World. You will be bound out as a servant. Your employer will pay me your fare."

"Can't you take me back to Bristol on your return trip?" Meth asked.

"Not without money," the captain said, but he promised to tell the innkeeper what had happened.

"I don't want him to think I was unhappy and ran away," Meth said.

Weeks on board the *Nancy Brown* made Meth long for land. Philadelphia was a small town on the edge of a wilderness, but he was glad to get there. The captain bound him out to a tavern keeper. In exchange for food and lodging, he was to work there until he was eighteen.

"Bound means you *must* stay," the captain said. I have promised you will, so no running away."

"Where would I run to?" asked Meth.

At first, Meth longed for the day when he could go home. But, as time passed, he came to like the New World. It was big. It was empty. Just the kind of place for a boy to seek his fortune. And so, on his eighteenth birthday, with the money the tavern keeper paid him and a new suit of clothes, that's what he did.

Historical Notes

In the deeds of an old house in New Britain, Bucks County, Pennsylvania, the builder—one

Methusala Evans—is stated to have come to America "by mistake," having been on a ship when it sailed.

In early Pennsylvania, orphans and destitute children, some as young as five, were bound out until the age of eighteen. On completion of their indenture they were usually given a small sum of money and a new suit of clothes. (From papers on early Quakers in Swarthmore College Library)

A Christmas Tree for Quentin

by Mary Ellen Pourchot

There would be no Christmas tree at the White House. Father had said so. And the Roosevelt children knew that when Father made up his mind, that was that.

"No tree!" cried eight-year-old Archie. "You'd think when a boy's father was President Theodore Roosevelt, his children could have a Christmas tree."

Father looked serious. "Our nation must stop this useless cutting of trees. We've started a new century.

It's time to change our ways and save our forests before they disappear."

"It won't be Christmas without a tree," said Quentin, who at five loved Christmas trees more than anything.

"I wish you could understand," Father said. "We must set an example to the nation. I know—I'll ask my chief forester, Mr. Pinchot, to come tonight to explain it."

The sitting room was gloomy when Father left. Quentin said he hadn't wanted any presents—just a tree.

"Maybe we could put our allowances together and buy one," Archie suggested.

"We wouldn't dare," said eleven-year-old Ethel. "Anyway, it's Christmas Eve. All the trees in Washington would be sold."

Archie stared from the window. It was almost dark. The trees made long shadows on the big lawn. One shadow, however, looked different. Could it be what he hoped for?

He sent Quentin out after some Christmas cookies. Then, pulling Ethel toward the window, he asked, "Didn't a man send a Christmas tree to the White House last week?"

"Yes. But Father said to send it back. We can't accept gifts from strangers."

"Look—against the wall."

Ethel gasped. "It looks like a Christmas tree. Archie, we could surprise Quentin with it."

"I'm going down to look. But first . . ." Archie glanced about. On the wall behind his sister, flames from the fireplace shone on Father's sword—the one he had carried at the battle of San Juan Hill.

"By buzzard," he breathed. "Just the thing. If the tree is too big to carry, I'll cut off the top."

"Shh! Someone's coming."

"Keep Mother and Father out," he warned, lifting the sword from the wall. He ducked behind the door as Mother walked in, then slipped out and down the servants' stairs.

Outside, a sharp wind stung his face. He stumbled across the dark lawn and fell over the big fir tree. It was hard to chop through the thick trunk. He tried a thinner place, swinging the sword up and down, often completely missing the tree in the dark. At last the top of the tree broke off. What he needed now was a rope.

Feeling like his Father must have at San Juan Hill, Archie charged up the stairs. At the top stood Father. Archie hid the sword behind his back just as Father turned around.

"Well, Archie, you're red-faced as a turkey. Dinner in eight minutes, on the dot."

"Yes, Father," Archie gasped. It was a close call. In the sitting room he returned the sword and asked Ethel to help find a rope. Ethel remembered that there was a lariat on Father's Rough Rider saddle.

"Bully!" said Archie. "While I go outside, you get the lariat and bring it up to my bedroom. Then, lower it from the window."

Archie stole down the stairs again and out into the dark. He heard the window open and the rope drop. Blindly, he felt for the noose and looped it over the tree. "Pull!" he called.

The rope jerked, the tree tilted, then soared to the window where it stuck.

Archie was panting when he reached his room. He and Ethel pulled the tree into his closet.

The deed was done. Would Father punish him for disobeying? Father always told them to be courageous, to do what they believed ought to be done.

"What do you think Father will do to us, when he finds out?" Ethel asked.

Archie stood straight and said he would take all the blame.

Mr. Pinchot arrived after dinner to answer the children's questions about Christmas trees. They all talked at once. Was it wrong to cut down trees? Were all of the forests going to disappear? Were Christmas trees bad?

Mr. Pinchot laughed. "What have you been telling the children, T.R.? You must have misunderstood me. Yes, the useless cutting of timber is a disgrace. But with proper cutting, we can thin a stand of trees and give others room to grow."

Archie grinned. "Mr. Pinchot, one shouldn't be wasteful of trees, should one? Especially if a tree is already cut and thrown away?"

"That's right, Archie."

Father said, "Perhaps the nation could grow Christmas trees in rows — like corn. We could plant fields of evergreens, so children in the future will always have trees."

"A bully idea!" chorused the children.

"I guess I was wrong about Christmas trees," Father said. "Now it is too late to buy one."

"We'll just have to dream about one," Archie said, trying not to giggle.

Later, when the family gathered before the sitting room fireplace for hot chocolate and Father's reading of "The Night Before Christmas," Ethel and Archie asked to be excused.

They disappeared into Archie's bedroom and didn't come back until stocking-hanging time.

Father said, "I hope your dreams are happy, children, even though we have no Christmas tree."

Quentin's lips quivered.

"Close your eyes everyone," Archie called. He and Ethel brought the little tree from his bedroom into the room. "Merry Christmas!" they both cried.

The shiny balls danced and tinsel glittered in the light of the fire. Father boomed "Ho ho, what a surprise!" and his laughter was as jolly as a Santa's.

But Quentin was speechless. He could only stare at this wonderful magical Christmas tree.

Voyage to Thanksgiving

By Janette Gentry

Ten-year-old Seth Hankins shivered. It was not yet morning and the cabin loft was cold. Hastily, he pulled on his leather britches, shirt, and moccasins. Then, with his bedroll of furs under one arm, he climbed down to the room below.

Ma stood by the fire tying the laces to her hooded cape. "Eat, Son," she said to Seth. "We mustn't be a hold-back to the others."

Seth took a spoonful of cornmeal mush from the iron pot cooling on the hearth. It was hard to swallow with the big lump in his throat. "I'm not hungry," he said.

Ma got Seth's coonskin cap from a wall peg. "'Tis sorry I am, son, that we have to leave at Thanksgiving time. But foul weather will set in soon."

"I know, Ma," muttered Seth.

Ma handed him his cap. "Come," she said, and carrying the iron pot, went out of the cabin.

Seth knew Ma was happy to be going to the new settlement. Pa had been a long hunter. Sometimes he stayed in the woods, hunting, for two or three months. Now he would be a farmer. Pa was already at the new settlement waiting for them.

Seth hated to leave Fort Patrick Henry, especially when it would soon be the time of Thanksgiving. For several days there would be much feasting, banjo picking, harmonica playing, and story-telling. And best of all, this year a schoolmarm would be arriving. There would finally be a school at Fort Patrick Henry!

Several children would be going to the new settlement. But not Seth's best friend, Wyeth Sutter. Wyeth had learned how to write his name before he came to the fort. Seth thought this was wonderful. Some people at the fort could write their names. But no one could read more than a few verses from the Bible.

Now, Seth could write Wyeth's name, too. He spent much time drawing in the sand—the letters and pictures of people and animals. He would rather do this than hunt or play ball, and he longed to go to school.

Dawn broke as Seth followed Ma across the frosty stockade yard. Reaching the gate in the palisade fence, he could see the two large flatboats waiting for those making the journey. Mr. John, the guide, had said it was easier to go around the rugged mountains by boat than to go over them.

Friends were saying good-bye. Wyeth was there, and he and Seth shook hands like the menfolk were doing. "'Tis a long way you're going, Seth," said Wyeth sadly.

Seth held back tears. "If you learn all the letters, Wyeth, send me a message by a long hunter. Maybe somebody at the settlement can read." He turned and went across a rough plank to a flatboat.

"More folks will join us where the river forks," Mr. John announced. "Hope to get there 'fore dark."

Using long poles, a man on each boat pushed the flatboats away from the bank. Polemen watched for floating trees, snags, and sandbars. They would pole the boats around these dangers.

The children spent the morning watching for animals on the river banks. They saw deer, turkeys, and even some bears. Seth was feeling very sleepy when Mr. John suddenly yelled, "Down everybody! Make haste!"

As Seth hit the deck, he saw a group of Indians coming down to the edge of the river. His heart sounded like pounding thunder in his ears.

Then Mr. John called. "'Tis my friend, Onocosta." He raised an arm in salute and the Indians saluted in return.

Soon after that, there came a "ha-loooooo" from far downriver.

"Ha-loooooo," Mr. John called back through his cupped hands.

"'Tis the others," Ma told Seth.

Two more flatboats came into view They were tied to trees that jutted out over the river. People on the bank bustled around a fire, and one man stirred a big pot.

After the new arrivals were welcomed, the man said, "Don't you children want to be with our children until it is time to eat?"

Seth had wondered what the children were doing on one of the boats. They sat in a circle. A red-headed, older girl was with them.

Now the girl motioned for the new children to come onto the boat. "My name is Rachel," she said, after everyone had found places in the circle.

"We'll learn everybody's name later. Now let's go on with the lesson."

Seth gasped. "Lesson? Are you a schoolmarm?"

Rachel smiled. "No. But I can read and write. Mr. Bean wants me to teach you all while we travel. Can you write your name?"

"No ma'am," Seth said. "But I can draw my friend's name."

"Show us," said Rachel. She handed Seth her stick and smoothed the pile of sand that she had been using.

Slowly, Seth drew W—Y—E—T—H.

"What is your name?" Rachel asked.

"Seth."

"Watch," said Rachel. She brushed out the W—Y, then drew a curvy letter. "This is an *S*," said Rachel. "S—E—T—H—Seth."

Seth couldn't believe it. He had already learned how to write his name!

"'Tis almost Thanksgiving time," Rachel said. "So let's learn to write *Thanksgiving*."

Seth was thinking happily, *"To be sure 'tis the time of Thanksgiving already. Won't Wyeth be surprised when he gets a letter from me."*

Soldier of Peace

By Patricia Curtis Pfitsch

In the spring of 1945, the American Army and its allies were winning the war against Germany. American soldiers were occupying the little villages along the Elbe River in eastern Germany.

"Josef! Josef! Come quick!"

The fear in his small sister's voice made Josef jump up from the plow he was oiling and run to the barn door. Eight-year-old Annie was charging down the narrow lane, her feet pounding in the dust, her bright plaid skirt billowing out in back.

Josef could feel his heart pounding as he waited for his sister. Germany had been at war since Josef turned six years old. He was twelve now, old enough to run the farm, old enough to know that in wartime people died. Was it his father? Was it his older brother, Franz?

As his frightened sister reached him, Josef took her by the shoulders. "Annie, quick! Tell me what has happened."

"An American soldier. At the factory. He has a club!" There were tears streaming down her cheeks. "He must be going to beat up the Uncles. Josef, you're the only one who can stop it."

Josef's face turned pale. *How could he stop an American soldier from beating up Uncle Karl and Uncle Erich?* he thought. But Annie was right. Only boys and old men were left in the village now. He would have to try to save the Uncles.

He ran to a shed and wheeled his bicycle into the sun. "You stay here," he called to his sister. He swung his left foot over the seat and started off.

When he reached the factory, he leaned his bicycle against a towering pile of wood beams stacked in the yard. His uncles used the wood to make the molds, which were used to make ammunition for the big German guns. He tiptoed to the back door of the workroom and peered around the corner.

The workroom was gloomy compared to the sunlit yard. There was only one block of small windows, on the east wall. An unshielded light bulb was hanging from the ceiling.

The Uncles were cowering on one side of the room, by the worktable. The American soldier was standing next to a lathe, a machine used to shape wood. In one hand he was holding a club, narrow at one end, but thick and powerful at the other. He wasn't hitting anyone with it. Not yet.

"You make it!" The American was yelling at the Uncles in German. "You make it!"

Uncle Karl trembled and shook his head.

Josef was fascinated in spite of the danger. The war had always seemed far away from his little village. No bombs dropped. No soldiers fought. Now, here was a real soldier standing not ten feet away from him. The soldier's dark green jacket looked worn, but the small silver bars on his shoulders gleamed and flashed as he moved. His brown boots were shiny in the dim factory light.

All at once the American caught sight of Josef. He said something in another language and motioned for him to come closer. For an instant Josef stood frozen, then he began weaving his way through the big woodworking machines. His heartbeat sounded louder than his footsteps on the concrete floor.

"What is your name?" asked the American. He spoke German very badly. Josef could hardly understand him.

"Josef."

"My name is John," said the American, smiling.

Why was the soldier smiling? Josef did not smile back.

The American touched his helmet, a green one with two silver bars on the front, and held out the club. Josef stepped back.

"I want. . . ," the American began. "I want your father . . . "

"They are my uncles," Josef corrected him.

"Uncles," the American repeated. "I want your uncles to make one like this. Can they?"

The American's German was terrible, but Josef was beginning to understand.

"What is it?" he asked, pointing to the club.

"Bat. A baseball bat," the American answered.

"Baseball bat?" Josef asked, shaking his head.

"Look," said the soldier, putting down the bat and pulling a wrinkled magazine from his pocket.

The words were in English, but there were pictures, all of young men in white or gray uniforms. Some held small white balls and wore huge leather gloves. In one picture, a man was hitting the ball with a club like the soldier's.

"Game," the American said. "Baseball. We need bats to play the game."

In a flash Josef understood. The soldier wanted them to make more clubs so the Americans could play a game called baseball. Josef couldn't help himself. He started to laugh. The Uncles and the American stood and watched him, smiles beginning to twitch at the corners of their mouths.

"We thought you would hit us with the club," Josef explained to the soldier between giggles. He picked up the club and raised it over his head, pretending to hit an imaginary person.

The soldier looked startled. Then he began to laugh, too. He took the bat, stepped away from Josef and the Uncles, and swung the bat level with his shoulder. "Like that," he explained. "You hit a ball." He handed the bat back to Josef.

Josef turned to Uncle Karl. "He wants you to make bats like this one. To play a game." He looked at the American. "Right?"

"Yes. Much wood outside. Right?" The American said something Josef didn't understand and Josef laughed again.

Josef handed the bat to Uncle Erich. "Can you make these with the wood for the shell molds?"

Uncle Erich took the bat. He passed it from one hand to the other, feeling the weight of it. He turned it, examining the shape. Then he nodded. "We could do it."

"Would you get in trouble?" Josef asked.

Uncle Erich shrugged. "Bats, shells. It's all the same. How many does he want?"

"How many?" Josef asked the soldier.

"Fifty. Maybe more later. OK?"

The Uncles nodded. Uncle Erich placed the bat on the worktable. Then he and Uncle Karl shuffled toward the back door to bring in some wood.

The soldier carefully straightened his helmet. "Thanks," he said to Josef. "Come watch us play, OK? I could show you how." He smiled.

This time Josef smiled back. "OK," he answered.

Maybe the war would be over soon, he thought. Maybe, even if Germany lost the war, Father and Franz would be home to help with the planting.

He waved to the soldier and hopped on his bicycle. He'd better finish oiling that plow!

This is based on a true story. At the end of World War II, in the little town of Tangermunde on the Elbe River, a small ammunition factory supplied the entire American Army with baseball bats during the summer of the occupation. The American soldier, Captain John Pfitsch, was awarded the Bronze Star for his efforts in using a shell factory for peaceable purposes.

A Kite
Called Union

By William G. Wing

The man who stepped off the stagecoach in
Niagara Falls, New York, was tall and thin, with a
high hat on his bushy hair and a Spanish cape
over his shoulders. Some of the village boys led
him to a local hotel, then gathered outside to dis-
cuss the visitor.

"That's Charles Ellet," said one boy. "He's one
of the world's greatest bridge builders. He's going
to put a bridge to Canada over the Great Gorge."

"Don't be silly," another said. "Nothing can get across the gorge."

A boy named Homan Walsh felt his face flush with anger. "We've got to try," he said. "This is 1848, the modern age. America is building up. We need an easy way to get across the gorge."

Homan didn't say it, but he couldn't imagine how such a bridge could be built. Even at the hotel, he could hear the constant thunder of Niagara Falls, where tons of water poured over high cliffs and rushed away in rapids through a cleft called the Great Gorge. It had scared Homan even to look at it when he first arrived from Ireland. At Whirlpool Rapids, near where they hoped to build the bridge, the water ran faster than any racehorse. No one could go into the gorge to build a bridge.

Inside the hotel, Mr. Ellet was saying to a group of men, "Of course, we can't build the usual kind of bridge. However, I have brought from Europe a new kind of bridge. It needs no support from below because—" he paused dramatically—"it hangs in the air!"

He drew a picture for the men. It showed that the bridge, instead of resting on stone or timber supports, would hang from cables above the river. It would be suspended—a suspension bridge, he called it.

Then he explained. To start building, a line would have to be stretched from the clifftop in the United States across the gorge to the clifftop in Canada. "The distance is too great to throw a line across," he said, "and no one can cross the rapids in a boat, carrying the line. How shall we get it across?"

All the men made suggestions. Some thought a steamboat strong enough to cross the river could be made, but Mr. Ellet said this would take too long and cost too much. "A cannon!" another man exclaimed. The line could be shot from one cliff to the other. Mr. Ellet said he had been thinking of using rockets.

When the talk died down, Oscar Fisk said he had a cheaper and simpler idea. He would tell it, he said, if the others promised not to laugh at him.

"Now, gentlemen," he said, "the instrument used will be the same kind used by Benjamin Franklin to draw lightning from the clouds—an instrument that any child can make in an hour. A kite."

Mr. Ellet's eyes glowed. "I see no reason this wouldn't work. All we need is to get one string across the gorge. Then we can tie to it a stronger cord, pull that across, and then stronger and stronger ropes until we can pull across a cable. Let's do it!"

"Good," said Mr. Fisk. "And I know just the lad who can."

Mr. Fisk had noticed sixteen-year-old Homan Walsh skillfully flying his kites near the gorge. Mr. Fisk quickly found Homan and told him about the idea. A special kite would have to be made, able to support more than a thousand feet of heavy string to stretch across the gorge.

Homan began work at once. He talked to his father about the design. After a while, his father said, "Homan, you're doing something more important than flying a kite. Your kite string will join together two of the greatest nations on earth, the U.S. and Canada. Your string will make a union."

Because the best winds blew from Canada, on the gorge's western side, Homan took a ferry that crossed calm waters farther down the gorge. He left home carrying a basket full of balls of string in one hand and his new kite in the other. He had found just the right name for the kite: the Union.

Homan set up his gear on the clifftop in Canada across the gorge from his village. His kite lifted quickly in the lively March wind. By late afternoon he was sure his kite had reached the U.S. side. Now he had to bring it down without letting the string drag in the gorge, where it might be cut by ice.

Crowds had gathered, and giant bonfires were built on both sides of the gorge to help Homan keep his kite in sight. But soon it was too dark to see, and Homan felt no pull on his line. The string had been cut and the kite was gone.

The ice had become so heavy that Homan stayed in Canada for eight days, but when he got home there was good news: the Union had been found! Homan raced to repair the kite and returned to Canada.

This time the kite sailed across and was caught by Mr. Ellet's workmen on the American side. Over the next few weeks, heavier cords and ropes were tied together until a strong cable was pulled across, uniting the U.S. and Canada. Using that cable, a bridge was built.

After Homan grew older, he moved to Nebraska. He left home by train, crossing the bridge that had been built because his kite, the Union, had flown a string across the Great Gorge.